This book belongs to

....

Love from Yeis & Charlie.

Dedicated to my husband Badger for his support, my family and friends, and most of all Jane and Mark who brought Charlie in to our lives.

AuthorHouse™ UK
1663 Liberty Drive
Bloomington, IN 47403 USA
www.authorhouse.co.uk
Phone: 0800.197.4150

Published by AuthorHouse 02/10/2016

ISBN: 978-1-5049-9964-9 (sc)
ISBN: 978-1-5049-9963-2 (e)

authorHOUSE®

Charlie Chuck-Chuck's
Duck adventure

Written by Gail Puttock
Illustrations by Gemma Denham

Charlie Chuck-Chuck was a Pup.
But as a Pup had little luck.

Charlie came one day to stay,
from a farm that was far away.

Charlie Chuck-Chuck loved to play,
in the garden all the day.

In the garden there was a pond,
full of birds, ducks and swans.

Charlie Chuck-Chuck the nosey Pup,
wanted to play with all the ducks.

To the edge he wandered by,
he made the ducklings flap and fly.

Charlie fell in to the pond,
scrambled round and bumped the swans.

The swans snapped at Charlie and he did squeal,
his little legs went like four wheels.

The Swans chased Charlie all about,
Charlie couldn't find his way out.

Charlie swam for all his might,
turning left and turning right.

Charlie Chuck-Chuck scrabbled out.
When his owner gave a shout.

Charlie NO his owner cried,
Charlie shook with the surprise.

Off he wandered all bedraggled,
the birds laughing at him like a gaggle.

Charlie Chuck-Chuck no longer plays,
near the pond where the ducklings play.

He likes the water and the ducks.
But not the Swans that pecked him much.

Charlie is a real live dog who lives with his family in the countryside.
He is a rather strange looking but cheeky,
and cute little pup, who's breed is a sprussell.

He is a cross between a jack Russell and a cocker spaniel.
Some people think, when you tell them he is a sprussell,
that it has something to do with Brussel Sprouts.

He lives with his two friends Katy May the
Dalmatian, who is a grand old lady now,
and Maxwell Stinker Pants a Jack Russell so
called because he likes smelly things
to roll in and always needs a bath.

Lightning Source UK Ltd.
Milton Keynes UK
UKRC02n1107131018
330409UK00010B/48